THIS IS A BORZOI BOOK PUBLISHED BY ALFRED A. KNOPF

Copyright © 2000, 2002 by Hachette Livre
All rights reserved under International and Pan-American Copyright
Conventions. Published in the United States of America by Alfred A.
Knopf, a division of Random House, Inc., New York, and simultaneously in
Canada by Random House of Canada Limited, Toronto. Distributed by Random
House, Inc., New York. Originally published in France as Gaspard à la mer
by Hachette Jeunesse in 2000. KNOPF, BORZOI BOOKS, and the colophon are
registered trademarks of Random House, Inc. www.randomhouse.com/kids
Library of Congress Cataloging-in-Publication Data: Gutman, Anne.
[Gaspard à la mer. English.] Gaspard at the seashore / Anne Gutman ;
illustrated by Georg Hallensleben. p. cm. Summary: Gaspard goes to
summer camp at the beach in the hope of learning to windsurf, but soon
discovers that he must first learn to swim. ISBN 0-375-81118-4 [1. Camps—
Fiction. 2. Swimming—Fiction. 3. Windsurfing—Fiction. 4. Dogs—Fiction.]
I. Hallensleben, Georg, ill. II. Title. PZ7.G9844 Gaq 2002 E—dc21 00-054957
First Borzoi Books edition: April 2002
Printed in France   10 9 8 7 6 5 4 3 2 1

ANNE GUTMAN · GEORG HALLENSLEBEN

Gaspard
at the Seashore

Alfred A. Knopf · New York

When my mom was buying a swimsuit for me, I saw some surfboards. It would be so cool to know how to windsurf, I thought. So I begged my parents to send me to a summer camp at the seashore. Finally they said, "Okay, Gaspard, okay."

On the train to camp, I sat between a boy named Victor and a girl named Valerie. Victor told us that he was a champion swimmer, and this summer he wanted to become a champion windsurfer. "I'm a champion swimmer, too," said Valerie. "Me too," I said.

When we got to camp, I found out that I was sharing a tent with Victor and Valerie and another girl named Nicole . . . maybe a big white dog, too.

That night I fell asleep right away.

I dreamed I was windsurfing . . .

. . . and I rescued my friend Lisa.

In the morning, we practiced windsurfing on the sand. It was easy, but our camp counselor, Mr. Duval, told us that it would be more difficult in the water.

After our lesson on the sand, Mr. Duval told us to take our surfboards into the sea. But that water was deep! And it had waves, too! It was nothing like the lake with knee-deep water back home. I was afraid because . . .

. . . I didn't know how to swim at all!
Everyone was in the water, and I
was still standing on the beach.
Oh, it was TERRIBLE!

But then I saw three little boys who were not going into the water either. They were telling Mr. Duval that they didn't know how to swim. I wasn't alone!

Mr. Duval told us not to worry. He said that the others didn't know how to swim last summer either. And he promised that by the end of camp, we would all be swimming champions.

We went to the pool to learn how to swim. I was a champion at hanging on to the kickboard and splashing.

When we returned to the beach, we had plastic rings. And I bet the kids who already knew how to swim were jealous . . .

. . . because my ring looked
like a shark!